To the children,
grandchildren and
great-grandchildren
of Elsa Atterberry,
a true Gram
who gave Glad Dreams.

The Five Mile Press Pty Ltd
1 Centre Road, Scoresby
Victoria 3179, Australia
www.fivemile.com.au

Part of the Bonnier Publishing Group
www.bonnierpublishing.com

© 2013 Bunnies By The Bay ®

First published 2013

Printed in China 5 4 3 2 1

Glad Dreams

The Five Mile Press

Cricket Island was a welcoming home
for a puppy who slept on a boat.
Longing to be a real skipper at sea,
little girls kept his dreams afloat.

Sissy and Sam were his very best friends,
they explored in the garden all day.
They watched over friends, no matter how small,
and were helpful in so many ways.

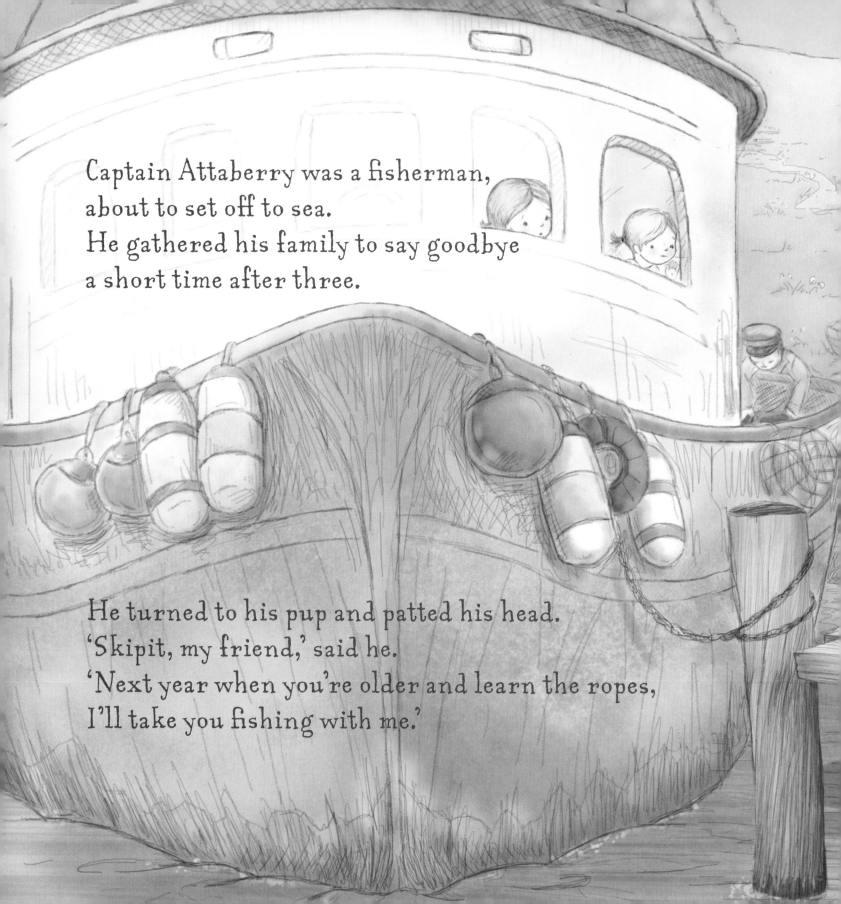

Captain Attaberry was a fisherman,
about to set off to sea.
He gathered his family to say goodbye
a short time after three.

He turned to his pup and patted his head.
'Skipit, my friend,' said he.
'Next year when you're older and learn the ropes,
I'll take you fishing with me.'

'But now I need you to guard my home,
my garden beside the bay.
Take good care of my family and friends,
for the time that I am away.

'Hold onto Blossom, reaching for posies.
She is very unsteady in boots.
And Bloom should tip-toe, when hiding in rows
of carrots and tender shoots.

'But most of all Skipit, watch over Bud,
he hates to lie down, I think.
He fusses and cries while rubbing his eyes.
dear Bud hardly sleeps but a wink.

'If you could help Elsie get bunnies to bed,
tuck them in with a story or two.
Lick them good night, snuggled up tight.
Skipit, I'm counting on you.'

Skipit playfully ran to the garden
'Let's make our own fishing boat!
Pretend we have sails, buckets and pails
and nets with bobbers that float!'

'Anchors aweigh!' they all gave a shout.
Emmit was now the First Mate.
High up the mast, Tad collected big bugs,
to be used for their fishing bait.

Then Bloom scratched her head and wondered aloud,
'Where are we sailing to, Bud?
I studied my map and looked through the glass
but I think we're stuck in the mud!'

Bud giggled with glee and hopped up and down
when he saw his silly friend Tad.
For this little green frog was caught in a pot,
pretending to be a
stone crab.

'Ahoy, little sailors!' Mama called from the hutch.
'Dinner is almost done.
Captain and crew, please don't forget,
that clean up can also be fun.

'The sun is setting, it soon will be dark.
It's been a big day with friends.
Time to drop anchor and lower the sail.
Today's journey has come to an end.'

Lily Mae leaped and was over the deck.
Emmie saluted and quacked, 'Aye Aye!'
'Tidy up sailors! Let's get things ship-shape
before we must all wave bye bye.'

But dear little Bud did not want to leave,
his tears were beginning to show.
He didn't feel hungry and just wasn't tired.
He whimpered to Skipit, 'No go!'

'Tomorrow, little buddy, is a brand new day,'
Skipit whispered in Bud's fuzzy ear.
'Go eat your carrots to grow big and strong
so we can go fishing next year.

'Now listen to Mother, hurry on home.
Sailor, I'm counting on you.
Go take your bath and hop into bed,
I'll come tell a story or two.'

After supper, Elsie filled up the tub.
'Time to clean our tummies and ears.
Places unseen need a good soapy clean
and try to shampoo without tears.

'Okay sleepy ones,' she finally said,
'to the sink to brush your two teeth.
Open up wide, brush side to side
remember to clean underneath.'

Skipit reported after making his rounds,
that all were happy and fed.
Holding soft blankies and favorite toys
everyone was ready for bed.

Sleepyhead bunnies drew close to his side
to hear a long Hareytale.
About a brave captain who went out to fish
but ended up catching a whale!

When the bedtime story had come to an end
there were only two things left to say.
'All aboard, sailors, say your goodnights
it's time for anchors aweigh!'

'Goodnight, Father, goodnight, Papa,
we hope that you can see the moon.
Goodnight, Captain. Goodnight, big whale
we hope to see you both soon.'

'Goodnight, baby Bud, have many sweet dreams
of sailing wherever you may.
Of boats and bait and pots full of crab,
you'll be a real captain someday.'

'Goodnight, darlings,' Mama said softy.
'May your Glad Dreams drift you to sea.
Many adventures await you there,
sail away, my dear sailors three.'

'Goodnight, Skipit,
you're our very best friend,
tell Papa that we have been good.

'Goodnight, Mama,' yawned three little ones.
'We'll stay in our beds like we should.

'Sleep tight, sweet Emmie and goodnight Emmit.
Pleasant dreams about catching fish.
See you tomorrow, Lily and Tad,
catching bugs for as long as you wish!'

'Goodnight everyone,' said Sissy and Sam.
'Tomorrow's a brand new day.
We'll see you aboard our good *Friend Ship*
In our garden down by the bay.'

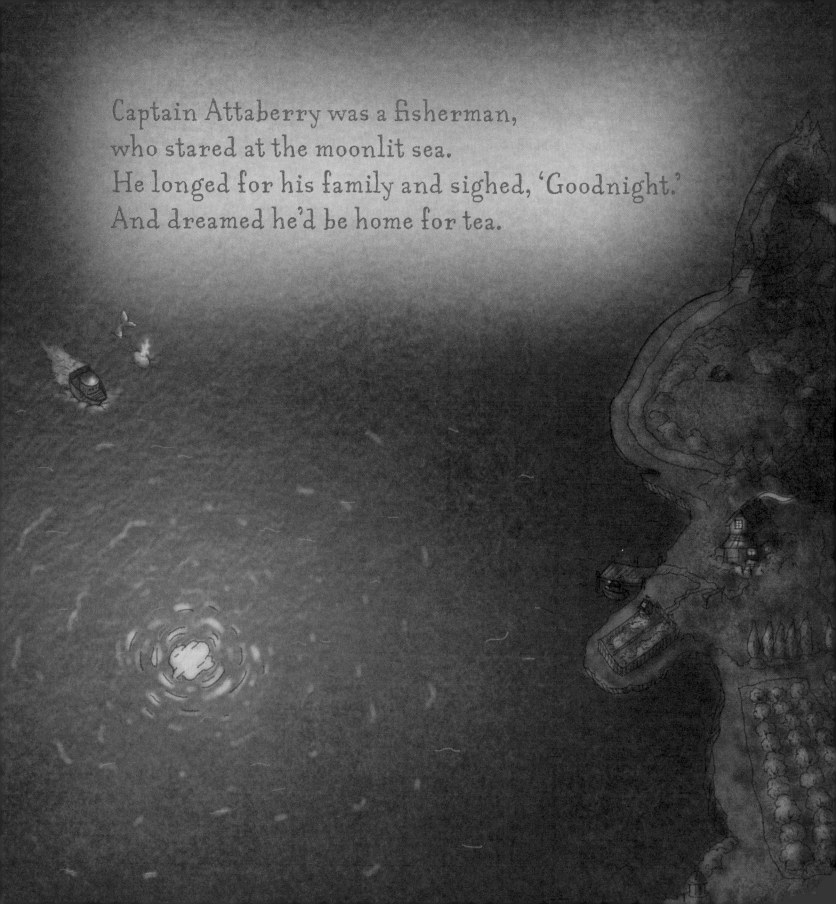

Captain Attaberry was a fisherman,
who stared at the moonlit sea.
He longed for his family and sighed, 'Goodnight.'
And dreamed he'd be home for tea.